Grandmother's Pictures

GRANDMOTHER'S PICTURES

By Sam Cornish

Illustrated by Jeanne Johns

BRADBURY PRESS
SCARSDALE, NEW YORK

1.917864

For Leda and Cora Keyes

Grandmother Keyes lived alone. None of her
grandchildren thought of her as being old; most
of them found it odd that their mother and neighbors
did not have fluffy white hair and drawn cheeks.
On the weekends when we went to see her, the early
spring turned all the streets into rows of green
trees and marble steps.
When she came to the door, I was afraid to kiss
her. After all, I was a boy. She would touch
my head saying that I needed a haircut. My heart beat
loudly, gladly when I came into her dark rooms.

In the winters when she was staying
in our house we sometimes found her in the
afternoon leaning over the stove
trying to keep warm; getting older
seemed to mean needing more heat.

In her rooms she kept a wood stove.
Coming by in the afternoon from school,
I sometimes chopped wood for her. Carrying
an armful of wood into the yard, I
would get on my knees and chop the wood
into pieces small enough to slip
into the stove. One day I missed the
wood and chopped off the edge of a finger.

She liked to be by the window in her apartment.
In the spring, birds whose names she did not know
were in the branches in front of the house. When
it rained the grandchildren would look out of
the window and wonder what happens when the bird's
nest gets wet and lightning is white in the sky.
In the room there was a book case, and records of
family births, my grandfather's shoes and a marble-
top bureau given to her by some white woman the
family had worked for. She believed in God,
and like most of the family, her
nights were dreams filled with visits from
members of the family.

"Before she died," said my grandmother talking about
her mother, "a giant bird flew into the room. He never
left the room, and no one could find the bird in the room."

Her brass bed like gold in the morning
moved from one member of the family to
another. I would sit up in the bed and
look through the bars feeling like a man
on a ship; the lights from the traffic
going across the walls, floors and ceilings
of the room, my body so small and brown in
those long and wide white sheets.

In her rooms there were oil lamps that
she read by at night and a green icebox with
a twenty-five cent piece of ice; an ice pick
she used to break me a piece of ice for
carrying in my mouth; a Bible one hundred
years old; flour, syrup and tea bags;
sometimes her wash hanging from the
clothesline in the kitchen.

One day I got into a fight
with the boy upstairs because
he said his father had the longest
blackest car in the neighborhood
and electric lights in every
room. Pulling down the shades
before she lit the oil lamp
to read, or closing the door of the room
where the lamp was lit, did not
keep any secrets from the neighbors.

She lived alone with photographs and scrapbooks
of her children and parents. Her curtains were newspapers
and the kitchen chairs were milk crates covered
with oil cloth. She was a tall woman, moving
through her three rooms, leaning over to avoid
anything that might be hanging from the ceilings.
She always had flypaper, clotheslines, and spider
webs crossing her rooms.

She spent most of her time by the window
watching the schoolyard, the traffic on
the corner, and the children in the morning
going to the high school up the street. She
was there most of the time clipping pictures out
of the Sunday paper we brought her every
Monday morning. I always wanted to ask her
about the pictures and the clippings,
but she never talked about them.

One day she looked at me and stopped cutting
pictures from the newspapers. Her eyes were
white behind her glasses as she opened up
a scrap book and started to show me the family.

My mother always said that to see me was
to see my father coming into the house.
In the pictures with his moustache like handles
on a bicycle, he stood with a group of men in
a circle, and all of them wore aprons. Behind
them were a long white fence and a few horses
standing still in the grass.

I could not see enough of him.

The sun on the clock and floor kept
me warm as she talked to me.

"Your father died after you were born, and
when you cried he would hit you on the
bottom." She asked me if I remembered
him, and I said, "No."

There was a picture of a woman sitting
on a porch, stiff and still, almost afraid
to smile. Her hands dropped into her lap,
the fingers in a tight grip.

"That is your Grandmother Nickols. She skinned
a cat and boiled him alive," my grandmother
said from a rocking chair, moving
back and forth in front of the light from
the window. Her hair growing white as straw and
dark as the unlit corners of the room.

*The house pictures opened on brick
streets, swept clean by street cleaners,
while black children arranged by height
stood in front of a doorway and tried
to smile. The faces were dots, the pictures
small. But still I noticed the hair thick
and curly, the women with collars up to
their necks with frowns in their mouths.*

There was a picture of my house, too, the screen
door opening up the darkness of the hallway and
the beginnings of the staircase. There was a lady
I remembered named Miss Carrol, married, widowed,
with a son named Henry who died in the war. She
stayed in her window reading the Bible, cursing
my mother and the children because we made so
much noise. She burned to death one Sunday while
ironing her clothes.

"The devil came through the walls of her apartment
and took her soul because the Lord did not allow
anyone to iron on Sunday," my mother said. This
had happened before in our neighborhood; this time the
devil took the woman and left a candle burning.
The candle burned until the preacher came and put it out.

There were many pictures of me. One was of me with my oysters on the table in the market, I had turned around and removed my hand from my mouth. The fingers were red with catsup. "Somebody had just said 'hello' and you were raising your hands in a hello of your own," my grandmother said.

One of the boys my mother used to play
with drowned when he went swimming instead
of going to school. I was glad we had his
picture. He seemed to be always near us
and none of us could forget him. Young,
in his brother's pants, curly hair like
a girl's surrounding his face, he looked
like he was getting ready for Sunday
School.

1917864

Before I could see all the
pictures, the streets were
quieting down for evening;
along the streets windows were
going down, the sounds of
newsboys. It was time for
me to go home through the darkness
toward my own house.

I wanted to take the pictures with me,
put them beneath my pillow at night;
let them touch my young face,
look again into the dark eyes of my
Grandmother Nickols.

I said goodbye, as children
say goodbye, quickly, as if
I neither had time to stay
nor cared about returning the next
day. She touched my head and said
my hair was long.

I walked home past the marble
steps, under the trees now
an evening green, with faint memories
of the child my mother and
father had put away
in pictures pasted and folded
by my grandmother's bed.

Sam Cornish, a major black poet now living in Boston, is the author of more than five collections of poetry. He has received grants from the National Council for the Arts, edited a little magazine and press and has published poems in numerous anthologies. GRANDMOTHER'S PICTURES is his second book for children.

Jeanne Johns, originally from Lancaster, Pennsylvania and a graduate of Bucknell University, now lives in the Massachusetts Berkshires where she conducts private lessons in fine drawing. For five years she operated The Loft Gallery of Lenox, which is now her studio. Her work is displayed in galleries in New England and New York City. This is her first book.